P9-BYS-886

The CURIOUS LITTLE KITTEN
Sniff Sniff Book

by **LINDA HAYWARD**
illustrated by **MAGGIE SWANSON**

GOLDEN PRESS • NEW YORK
Western Publishing Company, Inc., Racine, Wisconsin

Text copyright © 1983 by Western Publishing Company, Inc. Illustrations copyright © 1983 by Maggie Swanson. All rights reserved. Printed in the U.S.A. No part of this book may be reproduced or copied in any form without permission from the publisher. GOLDEN®, A LITTLE GOLDEN SNIFF IT™ BOOK and GOLDEN PRESS ® are trademarks of Western Publishing Company, Inc. The "Microfragrance"™ labels were supplied by 3M Company. Library of Congress Catalog Card Number: 82-80185 ISBN 0-307-13206-4/ISBN 0-307-63206-7 (lib. bdg.) A B C D E F G H I J

One day the curious little kitten was feeling *very* curious—much too curious to stay and play in her own yard.

She wanted to find out what
was behind all those other fences.
She wanted to explore all those
other yards.

Pit pat, pit pat. Through a white picket fence she went. And what did she find? Something pink and blossomy. THAT was a flower garden.

Scribble scrabble, scribble scrabble.
Through a hole in the wall she wriggled.
  And what did she find? Something wet
and sticky!
  THAT was fresh paint.

Skippity hop, skippity hop. On she went until she came to a wire fence.

And what did she see? Something thick and thorny!

THAT was a clump of raspberry bushes.

Plip, plip, plop. The curious little kitten jumped up on a railing and then plopped down to the ground.

And what did she find? Something poofy and powdery!

THAT was a pile of sawdust.

Scritch, scratch, scritch. Over a brick wall went the little kitten.

And what did she find? Something fresh and fragrant.

THAT was a bed of mint.

At last the curious little kitten came to a place where there were no fences at all.
And there she found something leafy and sweet! THAT was clover.

Then she saw something that made her more curious than ever—white boxes!

Pit pat, pit pat.
Through the clover she scampered.

The little kitten put her curious nose right up against one of those white boxes. *Sniff, sniff.*

She could smell something sweet and syrupy inside.

THAT was honey.

She could see something fuzzy
and buzzy flying out of the box.
THOSE were honeybees!
And what were those honeybees
after? Was it something furry and purry?

The curious little kitten
didn't wait to find out.
Scurry, scurry. She hurried
all the way home.

And there, in her own back yard, the curious
little kitten found something sweet and thick
and delicious!

THAT was cream.

And what did she do? She lapped it all up. YUM!